Getting Rid of ROBERT

by Alison Strickland
illustrated by Estella Hickman

For my brothers. . . Robert and David Ghen

Published by Willowisp Press, Inc.
401 E. Wilson Bridge Road, Worthington, Ohio 43085

Printed in the United States of America
10 9 8 7 6 5 4 3 2 1

ISBN 0-87406-210-1

Contents

My Awful Brother ROBERT

The morning sun streamed through Allie's bedroom window. She rolled over and yawned. Then she sat up quickly. "Rats!" she muttered. "I overslept. I'm going to be late for school."

Then she remembered. "I'm not late," she said to herself, laughing. "Today's the first day of summer vacation."

Allie stretched happily. It felt good to know she could sleep longer if she wanted to. But Allie was too excited to sleep anymore.

Wonder if Susie's up yet, she thought. Susie was Allie's new friend. She'd moved in across the street last month.

Allie loved spending time with Susie. Susie was almost a year older than Allie. She was already ten. Ten seemed a lot older than nine to Allie.

Susie seemed older than Allie. But they were both in the same grade. Next fall they'd be going into fifth grade.

Allie wanted to call Susie. She jumped out of bed and put on some shorts and a T-shirt. Then she ran downstairs to the kitchen and picked up the phone. She dialed Susie's number.

"Hello," said a sleepy voice. Susie had her own phone right beside her bed. Allie wished she had one, too. Then her awful brother Robert couldn't listen to her talking to her friends.

"Hi. It's me, Allie.
What are you doing?"

"I was sleeping." Susie sounded angry.

"I'm sorry. I didn't mean to wake you up." Allie felt embarrassed. "I just wanted to see what you were doing today. Let's do something really fun."

"Sounds good," Susie said. "Come on over. We can make some breakfast and decide what to do."

"Great! I'll be right over."

"Be right over where?" asked Allie's mom.

"Over at Susie's," Allie answered. "We're going to plan what we're going to do today."

"That's fine," said Allie's mom. "Just remember to include Robert. I have two books to read before my first class. My first class begins tonight."

"Oh, Mom, I already promised Susie. We want to do something special today."

"Allie, we talked about this weeks ago," said Allie's mom. Going to school is part of my job as a teacher. Watching Robert while I'm upstairs studying is your job."

"I know, but you didn't say your school started today," Allie grumbled. "Now the whole day is ruined because of Robert."

The back door slammed. Robert bounced
into the kitchen.

"Hi, Allie. There's no school today!"
Robert's high-pitched voice got on Allie's
nerves. "Except for Mom. She has to go to
school. What do you want to do today,
Allie?"

Allie frowned. She wanted to tell Robert to get lost.

Then her mother frowned at her. So all Allie said was, "I don't know what I'm doing today. Right now I'm going over to Susie's."

"Can I come?" Robert asked.

"No," said Allie, huffily. "I don't have to babysit you till noon."

"I don't need a babysitter," said Robert. "I'm seven years old and in the second grade."

Allie thought about saying something mean to Robert. Then she looked at her little brother. Robert stood there grinning. With his glasses he looked like a great big smiling owl.

"Guess I'll go play in my tree house. See you later." Robert ran back outside.

Then Allie's mom said, "I know you want to be with your friends. There are places near home where you can go while I stay here and study. You just have to take Robert along. You only have to watch Robert three afternoons a week."

"Okay Mom," Allie sighed. "I'll be back by noon."

2

Let's Dump Robert at the Movies

"I've got an idea," Susie said. "The new movie theaters are having their grand opening at the mall today. They're giving away free popcorn at the one o'clock shows. Let's go."

"That sounds like fun," Allie said quietly. She didn't want to tell Susie about taking care of Robert.

"There's a scary horror movie playing," Susie said.

"I can't go," Allie sighed. "I've got to take care of Robert this afternoon."

"That little jerk! How'd you get stuck with him?" Susie asked.

"My mom has classes at the university. She has to study to be a better teacher."

"Poor you," Susie said. "I'm glad I don't have a little brother. I'd hate to have to stay home with some stupid little kid."

Then Susie had an idea. "Why don't you dump Robert off at that other little kid's house. You know, the jerk he always plays with. He can stay there this afternoon."

"You mean Robert's friend, Davey," Allie said. "He's spending the summer with his grandparents." She followed Susie out the back door. They sat on the porch steps.

Susie looked determined. "Then we'll just have to find other ways to get rid of Robert."

"Mom said I can go places close to home," Allie said. "I just have to take Robert along."

"Would she let you take him to the movies at the mall?" Susie asked.

Allie was amazed. She never thought Susie would let Robert go with them.

"She might let us," Allie said. "I can ask. But she'd never let me take Robert to a scary movie. Horror shows give him bad dreams. What else is playing?"

"I don't remember. Let me check the paper again. There's that baby movie about the unicorn. I don't want to see that."

Allie thought she wouldn't mind seeing the unicorn movie. But she didn't say so. She didn't want Susie to think she was a baby.

"Guess we can't go then," Allie said.

"Wait a minute," yelled Susie. "I've got a great idea. We tell our moms we're going to see the unicorn movie. We send Robert in to see that one. Then we go to the movie we want to see. Okay?"

Allie's stomach felt funny. She knew her mom wouldn't want Robert watching a movie alone.

"I don't know," Allie said slowly. "My mom would kill me if she found out."

"Come on. It's no big deal." Susie looked impatient. "The little baby movie starts at the same time as the horror movie. They get out at about the same time, too. What could happen to Robert?"

"Nothing I guess," Allie said. "Okay, I'll go ask Mom if Robert and I can go."

As Allie ran home she worried. What if Robert tells Mom when we get home? she thought.

We Got Rid of Robert

"But I want to go with you," Robert complained. He and Allie were waiting in line for free popcorn. Susie had gone to buy their tickets. "You can't go with us. We're going to see a really scary movie. It would give you bad dreams," Allie answered.

"Then why don't you come with me?" Robert pleaded.

"Come on, Robert. You said you were too big for a babysitter. That means you're big enough to watch a movie alone," Allie said.

"What if I get lost?" Robert looked frightened.

"Your movie is over just a few minutes before ours," Allie explained. "You stay in your seat till I come in and get you."

Just before it was their turn at the popcorn counter, Susie joined them. "Here are the tickets. I made it just in time. The movies start in a couple minutes."

They walked down the long hall lined with movie theaters. "Here's your movie, Robert," Allie said. "Now remember. Wait in your seat till I come get you."

Robert didn't say anything. He took his popcorn and walked into the dark theater. When he disappeared, Allie felt butterflies in her stomach. She felt guilty, too.

"We got rid of Robert!" Susie said, laughing.

Allie just nodded as they walked into their theater.

4

Where's Robert?

"Wow! What a scary movie!" Susie said, as they walked up the theater aisle.

"I know," Allie added. "I bet I closed my eyes at least ten times!"

"Good thing Robert didn't come. He wouldn't sleep for a week!" Susie said.

When Susie and Allie got out of the theater, they went to where they'd left Robert.

"Wait here. I'll go in and get him," Allie said. Then she walked into the dimly-lit theater. The theater was completely empty.

"Robert!" Allie called. "Where are you, Robert?" There was no answer.

Allie ran back out into the hall. "He's gone! I can't find him!" she gasped.

Susie wasn't at all upset. "The little brat's probably hiding from you. Want me to look?"

Allie started biting her fingernail. "He's probably been kidnapped!"

"Calm down," Susie said. "Who'd want to kidnap a creep like Robert?" Then she grabbed Allie's arm. "We'll find him. Let's go to the lobby and see if he's there."

Allie and Susie ran into the lobby. There was Robert sitting on a bench eating popcorn.

They walked out into the sunlight. Robert kept talking about the unicorn movie. "When we get home I'll tell you the whole story." Susie rolled her eyes at Allie. She looked bored.

"Sure, Robert. We'll do that," Allie said. "Just don't tell mom I let you go alone. Okay?"

"Okay. I'm not a baby anymore."

5

You'll Never Find Us!

"No, Allie," said Robert. "You can't move yet. Not till the unicorn touches you with its magic horn."

Allie kept still. She waited for Robert to touch her with his cardboard horn. They'd made the horn out of a toilet paper tube. Then they'd covered it with cooking foil. She'd tied a rubber band to the horn so it would stay on Robert's head.

Just as Robert touched Allie with the horn, the phone rang.

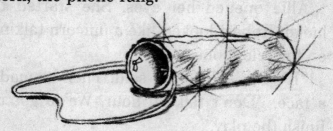

"Don't get up," Robert said. "The play's not over yet. I'll get it."

Allie opened her eyes. She started to laugh. Robert looked like a unicorn talking on the telephone.

"It's Susie," Robert said. Then he made a face. "Don't talk an hour. We've got to finish the play."

Allie took the phone. "Hi, Susie. What's going on?"

"Nothing," said Susie. "I'm bored. Since Barbie started her summer job, it's too quiet around here."

Barbie was Susie's teenage sister. Barbie had a driver's license. Sometimes she'd let Allie and Susie watch her put on her makeup. Allie couldn't wait till her mom would let her wear makeup.

"Why don't you come over?" Susie asked.

"I can't. I'm watching Robert."

"Darn! I forgot," Susie grumbled.

"I'm so bored," Susie said. "I'll come over even if Robert's around."

"I'm not allowed to have anyone in the house while Mom's studying," Allie said.

"Okay. I'll meet you outside in a couple of minutes. Bye." Susie hung up before Allie could answer her.

"It's about time you hung up," Robert said. "Now let's finish our play."

"I'm tired of acting out the unicorn movie. Let's go outside."

"Come on, Allie. Our play is almost over. You promised."

"We'll finish it later. Take off the horn and come outside," Allie said impatiently.

"It's too hot," Robert said, "and there's nothing to do outside."

"Come on, Robert. Let's go," Allie yelled. she was getting tired of taking care of Robert.

"Hi, Allie. Hi, Robert," Susie said cheerfully. "How about a game of hide and seek?"

Allie was surprised. She didn't expect
Susie to want to play with Robert.

Robert smiled and said, "Sure. Let's
play."

"You get to hide your eyes first,
Robert," Susie said. "Remember, you
have to count to a hundred before you
open your eyes."

"Okay." Robert leaned his head against the tree in their front yard. Then he began to count.

Susie motioned for Allie to follow her. She ran through the neighbor's backyard and headed down the sidewalk.

"Where are you going? This is too far from home," Allie said. "Robert will never find us."

Susie grinned. "Exactly. We're getting rid of Robert. We're going to get some ice cream."

Allie felt her stomach tighten. She didn't like to think about leaving Robert alone.

Three blocks later, they were at the ice cream store. Susie reached into her pocket and pulled out a handful of coins. "It's my treat."

"Thanks, but I can't," Allie told her.

"Why not?" Susie asked.

"I can't run away from Robert. I'm sure he'll tell Mom."

"That's why we played hide and seek, dummy." Susie laughed. "It's not our fault if he can't find us."

6

Go Away And Leave Me Alone!

When Allie got home, there was no sign of Robert. Her mother was in the basement doing laundry. She ran up the stairs and knocked on his door. There was no answer. She tried to open the door. But Robert had leaned a chair against it. Allie was locked out.

"Robert, are you in there?" Allie yelled.

"What do you care?" he yelled back.

"Come on, Robert. Open the door."

"You and Susie are mean." Robert
sounded like he'd been crying. "You ran
away from me. I hate you. And I hate your
dumb friend, Susie, too."

Allie remembered what Susie had said.
She told Robert the same thing. "It's not
our fault if you couldn't find us."

"You ran away from me on purpose!"
Robert screamed. "I don't want to play
with you anymore."

Allie sighed and went into her room.
There on her bed was Robert's unicorn
horn. It was wadded up in a little ball.

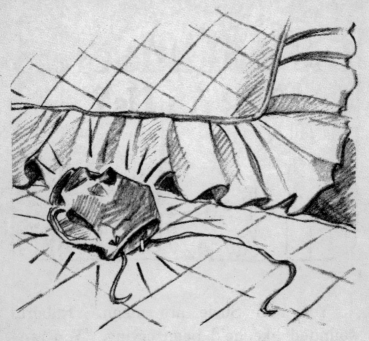

7

Did the Little Creep Tell on Us?

"So, did the little creep say anything to your mom?" Susie asked.

"I guess not," Allie said. "If he had told, Mom would have yelled at me by now."

Allie didn't like hearing Susie call Robert a little creep. She felt like telling her so. But she was afraid Susie would get mad at her.

"Hi, you two," Susie's sister Barbie said as she came in through the back door. "Guess what? The Summer Celebration Fair's going up in Holiday Park. That's only eight blocks from here."

"Oh, good," Susie answered. "Now we'll have something to do for a change."

"There's going to be a lot of fun things happening," Barbie went on. "There's a clown show and a cheerleading competition."

"Allie, we've just got to go," Susie said.

"Sure, I'd love to," Allie said. "I went last year. It was great. This year sounds even better. When's the Summer Celebration Fair going to open?"

"Friday, I think," Barbie told them.

"Oh, no, that's when you have to watch Robert, isn't it?" Susie asked, frowning. "We've got to figure something out."

What Will We Do with Robert?

Allie's mom stopped her car at the entrance of the fair. "Don't let Robert out of your sight," Allie's mom warned. She looked sternly at Allie. "Remember, I'll be at the library. Call me if you have any problems."

Then Allie's mom looked at Susie. "Are you sure your sister knows where to meet you?" she asked.

"Sure," Susie answered. "At the main entrance. She'll be there a little after five o'clock."

"All right," said Allie's mom. "I'll be home just a little before you."

Susie, Allie, and Robert tumbled out of the car.

"Have fun. And be careful!" Allie's mom called as she drove away.

The three of them walked to the ticket line. Allie reached into her purse for her wallet. All she had were two dollars. Then it hit her. She'd forgotten to get money from her mom.

"Robert, did Mom give you any money?" she asked hopefully.

"No. I thought you had it." Robert looked around excitedly. "Hurry up, Allie. I can't wait to ride the Ferris wheel."

"Oh, no! Now what are we going to do?" Allie was frantic. "We don't even have enough money to get in."

Susie counted her money. Then she said, "Robert, go see how much it costs to get in."

After Robert ran to the front of the line, Susie said, "I have enough for you and me. We could send Robert home."

"I don't know." Allie looked worried. "He's never walked that far alone before. What if he gets lost?"

"How could he get lost?" Susie asked. "It's only eight blocks."

"What's he do when he gets home?" Allie was nervous.

"Doesn't your mom always leave a key under the flower pot by the back door?" Susie asked. "All he has to do is let himself in. You leave early and walk home. I'll tell Barbie that you and Robert decided to walk home. Your mom will never know."

Allie still wasn't sure.

"Stop worrying," said Susie. "You're the one who forgot to get money. Now don't ruin my whole day because of Robert."

9

Don't Be Such a Wimp!

"Be sure to walk straight home," Allie told Robert. She gave him a nudge down the sidewalk. Robert waved sadly to Allie as he walked slowly away.

"See, Allie, I told you. No problem," Susie said. "Now let's go have some fun."

Allie swallowed hard. Her stomach felt funny again. Then she said, "I can't let Robert walk home alone."

"Don't be such a wimp," Susie said. "What could happen to him?"

"I don't know. But I'm leaving. You can stay if you want to."

"That's stupid, Allie," Susie said angrily. "You're acting like a baby."

"I'm going home." Allie turned and ran past the rides to the sidewalk.

It seemed like it took Allie forever to run the eight blocks home. "Please, God," she whispered. "I'll never do anything else wrong in my whole life. I promise. Just let Robert be safe."

Allie finally reached her house. "Robert, where are you? Robert, I'm home!" she yelled.

The house was quiet.

Maybe he's up in his tree house, she thought.

She scrambled up the ladder to the tree house. There was Robert. He was playing with his toy soldiers. He looked at her sadly through his wire-rimmed glasses.

"Robert, I never should have let Susie talk me into sending you home. I promise I'll never do anything like this again." Allie felt her eyes fill with tears. "I'm sorry, Robert."

"That's okay. You want to play army?"

"Sure," Allie answered. "I'll play anything you want."

10

Is Robert OK?

"Allie, Susie's on the phone," her mom yelled.

Allie took the phone from her mom. "Is Robert okay?" Susie asked.

"Yes, he's all right." Allie sounded serious.

"See, I told you there was nothing to get so upset about."

"Yes, there was," Allie said. "Robert is my responsibility when Mom's studying. I know you think he's a little creep. Well, how would you like it if Barbie treated you like a jerk?"

"I know," Susie said quietly. "That's what she said when she picked me up at the fair. Did Robert tell on us?"

"No," Allie answered.

"Robert's a pretty good little kid. Ask him if he'd like to go to the Summer Celebration Fair tomorrow. Barbie said she'd take us. And tell Robert that I'll never try to get rid of him again."